Mr. Big and Mr. Small

and Other Short Stories in Chinese

ISBN-13:9781696961530

Table of Contents

Mr. Big and Mr. Small 3

I'm on Top 22

Play with Me 34

For audio to this book and other supplementary material, visit tinychinesehomeschool.com.

大先生，小先生

Dà Xiānsheng, Xiǎo Xiānsheng

Tips for parents: Start slow. First teach these two characters:

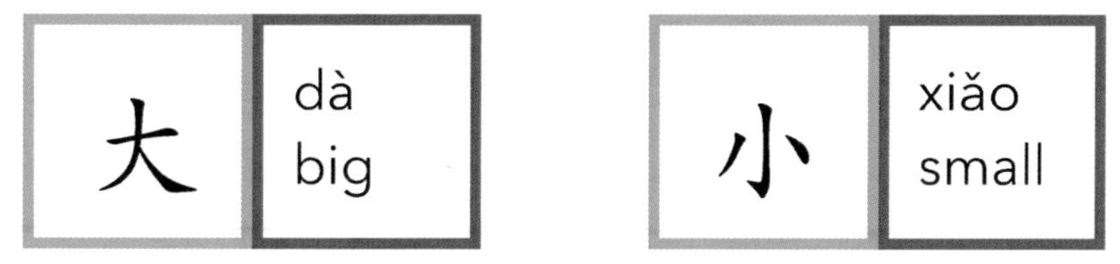

Parents can read the bulk of the story, but whenever you reach a character your child has learned, stop! Allow them to take over.

大先生

很大

很大。

Dà xiānsheng hěn dà, hěn dà.

Mr. Big is very big, very big.

小先生

很小

很小。

Xiǎo xiānsheng hěn xiǎo, hěn xiǎo.

Mr. Small is very small, very small.

大先生的

帽子

太小。

Dà xiānshengde màozi tài xiǎo.

Mr. Big's hat is too small.

小先生的

帽子

太大。

Xiǎo xiānshengde màozi tài dà.

Mr. Small's hat is too big.

大先生的

車子

太小。

Dà xiānshengde chēzi tài xiǎo.

Mr. Big’s car is too small.

小先生的

車子

太大。

Xiǎo xiānshengde chēzi tài dà.

Mr. Small's car is too big.

大先生的
房子
太小。

Dà xiānshengde fángzi tài xiǎo.

Mr. Big's house is too small.

小先生的
房子
太大。

Xiǎo xiānshengde fángzi tài dà.

Mr. Small's house is too big.

换帽子！

Huàn màozi!

Switch hats!

換車子！

Huàn chēzi!

Switch cars!

换房子！

Huàn fángzi!

Switch houses!

剛剛好！

Gāng gāng hǎo!

Just right!

Word List

dà	大	big
xiǎo	小	small
xiānsheng	先生	Mr.
hěn	很	very
tài	太	too
de	的	(possessive)
màozi	帽子	hat
chēzi	車子	car
fángzi	房子	house
huàn	換	switch
gāng gāng	剛剛	just/exactly
hǎo	好	good/right

Let's Review

Help Mr. Big find his way to his proper house by following the characters that describe him.

我在上面
Wǒ Zài Shàngmian

Tips for parents: Start slow. First teach these characters:

上面	shàngmian on top	下面	xiàmian underneath

As you read the story, do actions to signify "on top" and "underneath." Use hand motions to act out other vocabulary too.

我在上面。

Wǒ zài shàngmian.

I'm on top.

我在下面。

Wǒ zài xiàmian.

I'm on bottom.

小心！

不用擔心。

Xǐaoxīn!

Búyòng dānxīn.

Careful! / Don't worry.

我在上面。

Wǒ zài shàngmian.

I'm on top.

我在下面。

Wǒ zài xiàmian.

I’m on bottom.

小心！

不用擔心。

Xǐaoxīn!

Búyòng dānxīn.

Careful! / Don't worry.

我在上面。

Wǒ zài shàngmian.

I'm on top.

小心！

Xǐaoxīn!

Careful!

我在下面。

Wǒ zài xiàmian.

I'm on bottom.

Word List

wǒ	我	I
zài	在	be at
shàngmian	上面	on top
xiàmian	下面	below, under
xiǎoxīn	小心	careful
bù*	不	don’t
yòng	用	need
dānxīn	擔心	worry

*bù changes tones to bú when followed by a fourth tone.

Let's Review

Decide whether each object is dangerous or harmless. If dangerous, use your finger to trace a line from it to the sign in the middle. Make sure to say, "xiǎoxīn!"

跟我玩！

Gēn Wǒ Wán!

Tips for parents: Before reading, introduce the following people:

爸爸/bàba 媽媽/māma 哥哥/gēge 妹妹/mèimei

Bàba, gēn wǒ wán!

Daddy, play with me!

Wǒ tài máng.

I'm too busy.

Māma, gēn wǒ wán!

Mommy, play with me!

Wǒ tài lèi.

I'm too tired.

Gēge, gēn wǒ wán!

Older brother, play with me!

我太餓。
Wǒ tài è.
I'm too hungry.

Gǒugou, gēn wǒ wán!

Doggie, play with me!

Hǎo wán!

So fun!

妹妹，我們跟妳玩！

Mèimei, wǒmen gēn nǐ wán!

Little sister, we'll play with you!

Hǎo hǎo wán!

So, so fun!

Word List

bàba	爸爸	dad
gēn	跟	with
wǒ(men)	我(們)	I/me (we/us)
wán	玩	play
tài	太	too
máng	忙	busy
māma	媽媽	mom
lèi	累	tired
gēge	哥哥	older brother
è	餓	hungry
gǒu	狗	dog
hǎo	好	good
mèimei	妹妹	little sister
nǐ	你/妳	you (male/female)

Let's Review

Say the names of each line of people aloud. Complete the pattern by saying the next person in the sequence.

Answers:

Author and Acknowledgements

Author and illustrator, Enge Chen, was born in Taiwan and grew up in the U.S.A. She is a mother of three and loves to teach her children Chinese.

Thank you to Rebecca Chen, Summer Lin, Alexandria Despain, and Austin Van Wagoner for your excellent copy editing. Thank you to my daughter, Rosie, whose love of reading on her own gave me the inspiration for these books.

Need More?

Tiny Chinese Homeschool books are available through amazon.com. Worksheets, videos, and more can supplement your learning at tinychinesehomeschool.com.

Made in the USA
Las Vegas, NV
08 April 2021